MONTY
THE MAGICAL MAGPIE

THE FIRST
JOURNEY

BY
SUE TWEEDIE

ILLUSTRATED BY
MARJA BROWN

ISBN-13: 978-1-5272-3233-4

For

Isabelle

And all my wonderful friends and family who have helped bring Monty to life.

With Love x

THE FIRST JOURNEY

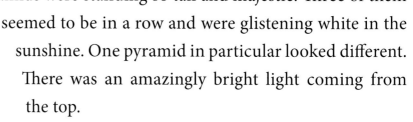

I T WAS A SWELTERINGLY HOT AND STEAMY EVENING, EVEN THOUGH IT WAS AUTUMN.

Melissa, sometimes known as Mellie Jo to her friends, was tossing and turning in her bed. She huffed and puffed, and throwing the covers off said to herself, "I'm too hot."

The lack of air was making her feel irritable and she needed a distraction. She kicked her legs off the side of the bed, tippy-toed over to the bookshelf and took out her favourite book – Stories of the Ancient Egyptians. She jumped back into bed, pillows plumped behind her, and began to read.

Mellie Jo very quickly became totally absorbed in the story of ancient Egypt, the land of the great pyramids. It was as if she were right there in front of them looking up. The pyramids were standing so tall and majestic. Three of them seemed to be in a row and were glistening white in the sunshine. One pyramid in particular looked different. There was an amazingly bright light coming from the top.

With the heat of the evening, she soon became drowsy. Her eyelids felt heavy and her eyes began to close, her head nodded to one side and the book slipped from her hands. Mellie Jo had nodded off.

All of a sudden came a tap, tap, tapping noise on the window directly above her head. The tap, tap, tap jolted Mellie Jo out of her sleepiness.

"What was that?"

With her eyes now wide open, she kneeled up on the bed and turned to face the window. She could feel her heart beating faster. There it was again – tap, tap, tap – louder this time. Mellie Jo gingerly moved closer to the window, close enough now to reach the cord attached to the blind. Taking hold of the cord, ever so slowly and gradually Mellie Jo rolled up the blind and revealed a stunning surprise!

"Oh wow! A bird on the windowsill outside!"

It looked sort of familiar.

Bewildered, Mellie Jo opened the window and the bird hopped onto the bedside table right beside her.

"Hello," said the bird.

"You can talk!" she exclaimed. "Whoever heard of a talking bird?"

"Of course I can talk!" the bird replied. "I am known as a magpie. Look at my shiny black feathers and my bright white breast."

The magpie smoothed his breast with his wings in a haughty manner.

"But magpie's breasts are black," said Mellie Jo. "You look like a waiter wearing a dinner jacket. What's your name?"

The bird replied, "Quirky, Fantastical, Thoroughly Fascinating, Mr Magical!"

Mellie Jo brushed her hair away from her face and replied, "What a blooming mouthful! Hmm, what shall I call you?"

With her hand on her chin and head cocked to one side, she said, "I know. Let's call you Monty, because it is a sort of grand name just right for a bird that looks so, well, shall we say … posh?"

"The magpie is a much-maligned creature as we are often accused of stealing shiny objects," said Monty.

"Whatever does that word maligned mean?" questioned Mellie Jo.

Impatiently clicking his beak and sighing, Monty replied;

"It is people that misunderstand us, and wrongly blacken our name. Although I look a bit different, I am a magpie nonetheless. But I am supremely extraordinary."

Mellie Jo began to feel excited and wondered how different this magpie could be.

"What makes you say that you are supremely extraordinary then?"

Monty stood bolt upright with his chest puffed out and replied, "For one, I live forever. For two, I have a wondrous warm personality, and for three I can take you on adventures you have only dreamt of, for I am magical."

"Would you like to come with me on a journey? A journey to a land not too far from here, where you can see a friend of mine who lives underground?" Monty asked.

"Oh yes please, but how on earth can that happen?" exclaimed Mellie Jo.

"I can take you there on my back! For I am very strong and magical, even though I may look small to you," replied Monty, puffing out his chest with pride.

He blinked one eye and clicked his beak and became just the right size to carry a passenger on his back.

"At your service mademoiselle!" announced Monty, making a deep bow so that his beak touched the ground at Mellie Jo's feet.

Both surprised and excited, she climbed up onto Monty's back. Mellie Jo threw back her head and laughed. What a strange sight this would be, she thought!

Whispering in Monty's ear, she said, "We must look crazy together – you so big! What if we are seen flying through the air?"

"Remember I am magical," he replied.

Monty took off with the greatest of ease. Mellie Jo felt the cool breeze on her face as they flew through the air

"This is wonderful – freedom!" she exclaimed to her new-found friend, Monty.

"I am exceedingly aware that this is your first adventure with me, so I am taking you to a place very close by, somewhere that you will be very familiar with," said Monty.

With Mellie Jo on his back, Monty beat his wings very slowly and they landed softly on the ground. Mellie Jo found herself in the woods that she knew so well. Nanny would bring her here all the time.

Sliding off Monty's back, Mellie Jo felt the leaves crunch beneath her feet. The leaves were beginning to pile up on the woodland floor and the smell of damp leaves hit her nostrils.

"Oh Monty, I know exactly where I am but what can you show me that I haven't already seen?"

"Well," said Monty, "I know that you have been shown the mounds of earth that a splendid little creature called a mole makes. I am going to take you inside and under the mound to meet a friend of mine."

"How do you know I have already been here?" replied Mellie Jo.

"Because I am magical, remember, and that means that I know many things that others may not know," Monty replied.

They found a mound covered in leaves and looked at it closely.

"This is it." Said Monty, "But we will need something to show us the way." With yet another click of his beak, Monty had produced a beautiful shimmering white light on the top of his head.

" This will be perfect, to illuminate our way underground," he said, lifting up his chin proudly. So as not to make too much disturbance, Monty whispered in Mellie Jo's ear,

"Let's go underground and meet my friend the mole in her home. Hold my wing and you will see how easy it is."

With that, they both became small enough to go inside the mound.

"Be very quiet for we don't want to frighten her as she has made this lovely place her home."

With a click of his beak, both Mellie Jo and Monty were inside the mound.

"Isn't this a marvellous place, with its tunnels going all over the place?"

Monty shone the light along the tunnels as he led her deeper underground.

In next to no time they were right in the heart of the tunnels.

"Shh! She's just over there!" said Monty.

Monty gently moved aside so that Mellie Jo could see.

"Oh my word, what a cosy little nest she is sleeping on! She is so pretty and what enormous front feet!"

"All the better to dig those long tunnels with, my dear!" Monty exclaimed.

Mellie Jo looked on in awe.

"She has such tiny little eyes."

Hesitantly, for Mellie Jo did not know if the mole could speak, she turned her head towards the mole and asked, "What is your name?"

The mole replied, "I am Molly. I knew you were coming to visit me while you were still above ground in the woods. I could feel the ground move and I could smell you."

"Ooh, you can talk, just like Monty!" she exclaimed. "How come your eyes are so small and yet you can dig such amazing tunnels?"

With a little voice Molly gently replied, "It's OK, for I do not need good sight as I live underground where it is dark. But I do have an extraordinary sense of smell. I have special little things on my snout called sensors that help me to find my food and my way around underground."

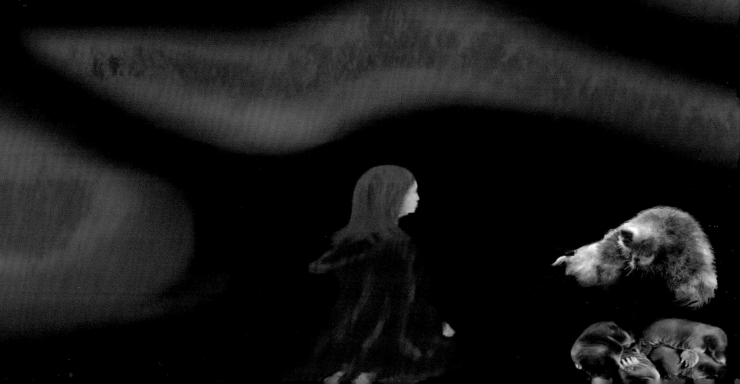

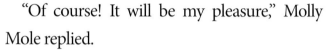

Lifting up a foot to show Mellie Jo, Molly continued, "And as you have already noticed I have big feet that allow me to shovel the earth with the greatest of ease."

Mellie Jo moved a step closer and asked, "Molly, please can I touch you, your fur looks so soft?"

"Of course! It will be my pleasure," Molly Mole replied.

Mellie Jo touched Molly very gently.

"Your fur feels like water, all silky."

It was if she was stroking something almost invisible, it was so utterly smooth and soft and Molly Mole was wonderfully warm.

Then Molly Mole, with a sigh, said, "Like your friend Monty, I too am a much-misunderstood creature that lives underground because above grounders' who call themselves human, don't much like the piles of earth that we make as they pop up in farmers' fields and sometimes appear on their neatly mown lawns!"

"What do you eat for breakfast?" asked Mellie Jo.

"All sorts of grubs and worms," Molly replied.

Mellie Jo continued, "What do you have for lunch?"

To which Molly Mole replied, "Worms and more grubs."

Surprised, Mellie Jo asked about dinner, to which again she replied, "Worms and grubs!"

"Is that all? And whatever is a grub? Sounds a bit boring," sighed Mellie Jo.

"A grub is an insect in the making, a larva to be more precise. It may become a beetle, or it may become something that flies like a daddy long legs," said Molly. "This is best for moles and there are plenty. What humans don't realise is that I actually help them. I eat the little grubs that eat the roots of plants. If I did not eat the grubs, more plants would die. I am actually a plant lifesaver."

"Do you have babies?" asked Mellie Jo.

"Oh yes!" Molly Mole replied. "They are here beside me, but they will leave home very soon and make burrows of their own."

Moving gently to one side Molly allowed Mellie Jo to take a closer look. Baby moles are called pups. They lay cuddled against each other fast asleep and were almost as big as Molly. Not wanting to disturb their sleep, Mellie Jo looked on in silence. These babies are very special because they were born very late in the summer. Some of my babies were born in the spring and have already left, but these sleeping beauties, will leave home very soon and make burrows of their own just like their brothers and sisters."

"What an unusual home you have, I live above the ground in a house. It is quite complicated compared to your lovely cosy simple home," Mellie Jo replied.

"My needs are met every day, I want for nothing and I am very content," exclaimed Molly.

Mellie Jo wanted to explore the whole burrow amongst the roots of the trees. It was a truly different world than that above ground.

It was difficult to tell how late it was, but Monty sensed that it was time the exploring stopped. With that Monty said, "Come on young lady, it is time you returned to your own home. For it is quite late enough."

Mellie Jo resisting replied, "No Monty, I am having such a good time – I'm staying!"

"Absolutely NOT!" he exclaimed with great authority. "We must not overstay our welcome and besides it is way past your bedtime."

With a deep sigh, Mellie Jo bowed her head and reluctantly agreed. She turned towards Molly and said, "Can I come and see you again, Molly?"

"It would be lovely to see you again, my dear. You could bring a friend if you wish and I can show you more of my world here underground," replied Molly.

"Thank you. It was such an adventure visiting you and seeing just where you live. From now on I will remember the good that you do in the fields and the gardens."

Mellie Jo turned to Monty

"OK, Sir Monty – let's go!"

"Yes indeed. It was so wonderful to show you the underground world of my friend Molly Mole," he replied.

"Bye bye Molly, I am going home now, but I will always remember my first adventure with Monty, flying through the air and coming down here to see you," said Mellie Jo.

"Hop on my back and let's take to the skies once more."

She jumped onto Monty's back and he whisked her away. Feeling the cool breeze on her face, with her hair flowing behind her, they were soon back home on the windowsill. They sneaked into the room through the open window.

"That was so amazing, thank you."

"I am so happy that you enjoyed the adventure. Where would you like to go next time?" asked Monty.

"Another adventure? How exciting!" replied Mellie Jo.

Mellie Jo glanced over at the book she had been reading before Monty arrived.

"I know! Egypt, to see the pyramids. That would be amazing!" she replied.

With that, Monty leapt onto the windowsill.

"That sounds very exciting to me. Goodnight my fair friend, 'til next time." And he flew off into the moonlight.

Mellie Jo cried after him, "Goodnight Monty! Come again soon please." Realising that actually she was exhausted after her adventure, she laid her head on the soft puffy pillow and before you could say Jack Robinson she had fallen fast asleep.

THE END

A BIT ABOUT THE AUTHOR

Born and brought up in Wiltshire Sue has always had a love of nature and being outdoors. Whilst walking her daughter's Springer Spaniel in the fields and woods near the Kennet and Avon canal close to her home in September 2016, she was inspired to write children's stories. The titles of 10 books revealed themselves and the first one in its entirety was written in no time. The stories are based around bedtime stories that were told to her children when they were young. The central character being a magical bird called Monty Magpie. Sue's granddaughter Isabelle now too loves the adventures that Monty takes her on.

A BIT ABOUT THE ILLUSTRATOR

Marja Brown studied art at Marnix College Holland in the 1960's and began her creative career as a successful potter exhibiting at the Chelsea Flower Show. Marja then changed direction and trained as a therapist and worked in this field for many years. Retiring at the age of 60 Marja felt compelled to return to the creative arts and began painting, particularly the local landscapes, seascapes and also her love of poppies. Playing with colours and textures, creating semi-abstract art is now filling her life. She successfully sells her paintings through commissions, exhibitions, craft markets and online galleries. Marja's artistic talents took her in a new direction in 2017 when Sue asked if she would illustrate a children's book and what you see is the end result of what is to be the first of many.

www.marjabrown.com

A donation from the net profit of this book will be made to the Wiltshire Wildlife Trust